AIR SHOWS

From Barnstormers to Blue Angels

By Elizabeth Van Steenwyk

A First Book
Franklin Watts

A DIVISION OF GROLIER PUBLISHING

NEW YORK   LONDON   HONG KONG   SYDNEY
DANBURY, CONNECTICUT

For Bob, my favorite pilot, his co-pilot, Cathy,
and their crew, Daniel and Andrew.

Photographs ©: AP/Wide World Photos: 55 (Steven Senne), 43, 45; Corbis-Bettmann: cover bottom, 1 bottom, 19, 41; Courtesy of the Arizona Aerospace Foundation: 9; Jim Koepnick: 49; L. Abrams: 58; Library of Congress: 7; Minnesota Historical Society: 25 (Swenson Studio); North Wind Picture Archives: 12; Peter M. Bowers: 16, 23, 26, 27, 28; San Diego Aerospace Museum Archives: 20, 22, 31, 34, 36, 42; Smithsonian Institution, Washington, DC: 13, 29; Superstock, Inc.: cover top, 1 top, 21; Team Husar: 51 bottom; The Western Reserve Historical Society: 37, 39, Tony Stone Images: 51 top (Andras Danes), 57 (David Frazier), 10, 14, 17 (Hulton Getty), 56 (Ross Harrison Koty), 52, 53 (Joe McBride), 50 bottom (Jean Pragen); TSW-Los Angeles, Ltd.: 50 top (George Hall); UPI/Corbis-Bettmann: 46.

Visit Franklin Watts on the Internet at:
http://publishing.grolier.com

Library of Congress Cataloging-in-Publication Data

Van Steenwyk, Elizabeth
Air shows : from barnstormers to Blue Angels / by Elizabeth Van Steenwyk.
p.   cm.—(A First book)
Includes bibliographical references and index.
Summary: Describes the history of air shows from the first air races to modern events.
ISBN 0-531-20294-1 (lib. bdg.)   0-531-15923-X (pbk.)
1.Air shows—Juvenile literature. [1. Aeronautics—History.
2. Air shows. 3. Stunt flying.] I. Title. II. Series.

TL504.A1V36 1998
797.5—dc21
[B]
98-20450
CIP
AC

Contents

INTRODUCTION

For five years, Wilbur and Orville Wright's first powered flight at Kitty Hawk, North Carolina, on December 17, 1903, remained virtually unknown. Few people witnessed the flight, and only three newspapers ran the story—all inaccurately. Most people had little knowledge of *aeronautics*—the science of aircraft flight—and most were doubtful that manned flight could ever be achieved. For the moment, the Wright brothers didn't mind the lack of attention. Their first airplane, though successful, was not very practical. Its longest flight had lasted only 59 seconds. The Wright brothers were content to work in relative secrecy, refining their airplanes until they could present the world with a more impressive model. Few people realized it at the time, but the age of flight had begun.

In 1908, airplane flight finally captured public attention. The Wright brothers unveiled a plane capable of staying airborne for more than an hour. Earlier that year, a group of men headed by Glenn Curtiss (a young aeronautics entrepreneur) and Dr. Alexander Graham Bell (the inventor of the telephone) also built and flew airplanes. Experimenters in Europe also demonstrated successful flying machines. Nevertheless, there was little organization and no planning in the direction this new science would take. The world was poised for action and waiting to see what would happen next.

The Wright Brothers' first flight at Kitty Hawk, North Carolina

1
THE SPEED CHASERS

I n 1909, the U.S. War Department offered a contract to the first individual or company who could build a flying machine that would travel 40 miles (64 kilometers) per hour for a distance of 5 to 8 miles (8 to 13 km). Motivated by this contest, inventors and engineers of all kinds set out to establish the first records for speed and safety. The Wright brothers' years of research had given them knowledge and experience far superior to that of their competitors. On July 30, 1909, Orville Wright demonstrated a plane that easily met the requirements of the War Department and won the contract. During the years immediately following, the aviation business took off around the world as other inventors and experimenters contributed their efforts to the new technology.

Made of wood and wire, a typical plane had two front wings, one above the other. This design is called a biplane. That any of these early planes could be considered safe or fast is a testament to people's imagination. The whole plane balanced on a tricycle undercarriage while its engine averaged no more than 50 horsepower. The pilot perched unprotected in the center of the lower wing. He seldom had a seat belt, and his passengers never did.

Orville Wright successfully demonstrates an airplane to U.S. War Department on July 30, 1909.

Early airplanes crashed frequently, putting the unprotected
pilots in jeopardy. Fortunately, the low flying speeds of
these planes made crashes a little less dangerous.

Off to the Races

Small, informal air races quickly developed. It took only two planes and two pilots. In the United States, James Gordon Bennett, son of a pioneering publisher, had conducted automobile and balloon races since the turn of the century. He had hoped to stage the first international air race, but organizers in France beat him to it. Bennett did, however, sponsor a race at the event. He offered a $5,000 prize and trophy to the pilot who completed the fastest two laps around the 10-kilometer (6.2-mile) course.

Twenty-eight pilots from around the world entered this race in Rheims, France, on August 22, 1909. One hundred thousand spectators showed up to watch it on the first day. Unfortunately, it had been raining most of the night. Now, as the event began, planes sputtered across the field to take off, only to become hopelessly stuck in the mud.

To most of the spectators it didn't matter much what the planes or pilots did. Few had seen a plane fly or even been that close to one before, so just being there was enough. The aircraft managed to take off a couple of days later, and some even completed laps around the course. Glenn Curtiss turned in the fastest two-lap time and won the first James Gordon Bennett Trophy.

Glenn Curtiss won the first James Gordon Bennett Trophy in Rheims, France, in 1909.

Soon the spectators were so busy watching near misses and rough landings that Henri Farman's record-setting flight for endurance was almost overlooked. When he finally bumped down to a landing after his eighteenth lap, he had flown a record 111 miles (179 km) in 3 hours and 56 seconds. Momentarily paralyzed by his prolonged exposure to cold and wind, Farman couldn't even climb out of his plane. He had to be carried to a hangar where he later revived.

In October 1910, Bennett sponsored an American air race at Belmont Park, New York. Aviators came from around the world. One pilot set a speed record for the 100-kilometer (62.1-mile) course, averaging 66 miles (106 km) per hour. Another aviator, Arthur LeBlanc, hoped to break that record with his aircraft. Entering the last lap of the race, his plane suddenly sputtered and quit. A gust of wind threw the plane into a telegraph pole, shattering the plane and breaking the pole in half. LeBlanc walked away without serious injury, but his chance to break a speed record was shattered along with his plane.

**Henri Farman rounds a course marker on
August 23, 1909, in Rheims, France.**

This plane, piloted by Maurice Prevost, won the first Schneider Maritime Competition in Monaco in 1913.

The Jacques Schneider Maritime Competition would become one of the biggest and best in air-racing history, but the first one, held in Monaco in 1913, gave no indication of its future greatness. Obsessed with finding a seaworthy airplane, Schneider required all entries to cover a distance of 500 meters (1,640 feet) "in contact with the sea." Schneider's quest for reliable seaplanes was a valid one, especially because airports were very rare. It was easier and less expensive to land a plane on water than on land.

Unfortunately, the planes seemed to spend more time on, or in, the water than in the air. They bounced across the surface of the sea and waterlogged their own engines. One dived, nose first, into the ocean, never to be seen again. Seaplane design had a long way to go.

Preparing for War

As air races became more common, governments around the world became more interested in the possible military uses of airplanes. In an effort to gather information for war purposes, European governments quickly began to sponsor their own air races. By the outbreak of World War I in Europe in 1914, Germany and France each had built several hundred planes for military purposes. Yet the United States remained neutral and unprepared for conflict. Some Americans worried that should the United States be drawn into the war, the U.S. military would be unprepared to attack or defend itself in the air. Some Americans decided to take matters into their own hands.

On a hot September afternoon in 1914, the members of Congress were startled to see a wood-and-wire biplane *buzzing* the Capitol. Congress adjourned to watch an amazing air show performed by pilot Lincoln Beachy. Beachy circled the Capitol and then the Washington Monument.

Finally, Beachy landed on the White House lawn and waited until the authorities and the press caught up to him.

Lincoln Beachy is pictured here racing an automobile around a track. In 1914, Beachy made headlines by flying an airplane around prominent landmarks in Washington, D.C.

Then he pointed out to everyone that an airplane from another country could easily do what he had just done because the United States couldn't defend itself in the air.

Later it was announced that Beachy had been invited by the secretary of war to demonstrate the inadequacy of American defenses against an air attack. The publicity stunt worked. Soon, the United States began a preparedness plan that included air defense. By the time the United States entered World War I in 1917, factories were already turning out thousands of planes. The military aggressively trained young pilots to fly them.

At the end of the war, 767 American combat pilots and nine thousand more soldiers with some flight training returned to civilian life. The prospect of returning to former jobs bored these new pilots used to the excitement of wartime training and flying. The new aircraft industry had a surplus of airplanes, and they marked them down to sell. It didn't take long for the abundance of pilots and the abundance of planes to come together to form a new kind of American entertainment. It was called barnstorming.

British planes (with circles on wings) fight German planes (with crosses on wings) during World War I.

2
GYPSIES OF THE SKY

The airplane of choice for most barnstormers was the Curtiss Jenny. By the end of World War I, a New York state airplane factory owned by aeronautics entrepreneur Glen Curtiss had turned out more than six thousand of these cheap training planes. Thousands more were manufactured before the government ended its contract with Curtiss. Mostly a product of trial and error, the Jenny, as it was called, was often described as "a bunch of parts flying in formation." Nevertheless, it was a giant step forward in aircraft design. And despite its limitations, the Jenny was the favorite among barnstormers.

Like all aircraft of the day, the Jenny had no brakes. Pilots landing too fast risked hitting fences or anything else standing in the way. In an emergency, they learned to aim at haystacks or fly between two trees. The haystacks gave a soft landing, and the trees tore off the

A Curtiss Jenny rests in a farmer's field.

wings, dissipating the energy and forward motion of the craft. Usually, the pilot walked away unharmed.

Because these planes spent their lifetimes outdoors in all kinds of weather, they needed constant attention. The pilot became his own mechanic, and oftentimes designer as well, constantly trying to repair problems from continued wear and many wrecks. The pilot-mechanic learned to patch the body of the plane, called the fuselage, with extra fabric and pieces of packing crate.

While flying, a pilot kept a special eye out for cows. These animals acted as weather vanes because they turned their tails to the wind. Once the plane landed,

Barnstorming was a dangerous activity. Pilots learned to fix their planes after a crash—if they survived.

however, cows were to be avoided. If planes were left untended in an open pasture, the cows licked the nitrate dope (used as glue) from the wings, leaving surfaces dangling loosely from the wooden framework.

The pilot also watched for garages as he flew because they were his only source of fuel in the back country. The distance he landed from a garage was the distance he carried his gasoline back to his aircraft. Rural airports had not yet been invented.

The pilots called themselves barnstormers because they usually landed in cleared areas of farmland, near barns. The aviators tried to interest farmers and villagers in going for a ride by buzzing the area a couple of times. If no one paid any attention, the pilots moved on. If the townspeople and farmers followed them to the nearest pasture, however, the pilots knew they could feed themselves and fill their tanks with money earned from paid-for rides.

The flyers presented themselves as dashing, romantic figures, often dressing in fancy riding boots, a white silk scarf, and a typical aviator's uniform. Soon, as the novelty began to fade, they needed more than dashing appearances to draw a crowd. Barnstormers began to add stunts to their shows.

Barnstormers dressed in glamorous aviation uniforms, often complete with a white scarf.

**Soon, barnstormers added daring stunts
to their routines to attract larger crowds.**

Ormer Locklear

Ormer Locklear was one of the first barnstormers to become a national celebrity. Willing to perform despite "rain, shine and cyclone," Locklear would jump from a speeding car to a rope ladder attached to an airplane overhead, and then climb into the plane itself. He transferred from plane to plane in midair, and walked on the wings of planes in flight. He caught the attention of moviemakers with his daredevil stunts and soon became a star attraction in that new form of entertainment as well. However, during the grand finale of a movie he was shooting, Locklear was killed on August 2, 1920—a brief year and a half after he began his career. But he'd left his mark on the public. More than 50,000 people lined the streets of Fort Worth, Texas, to watch his funeral procession, and over 15,000 went to the cemetery to see him buried.

Locklear's death caused headlines around the world. An article in the *Los Angeles Times* mourned the death of "such fine young men" as Locklear but added that "their loss is not likely to deter other audacious young fliers."

And it didn't. More and more barnstormers took to the air. Some flew planes that could be kept level only by leaning to the side while seated at the controls.

Ormer Locklear performs a handstand on the wing of a Jenny.

Other planes had to be bounced off knolls on the runways to get them airborne.

In 1922, a young American pilot named Charles Lindbergh enrolled in the Nebraska Aircraft Corporation flying school to learn to fly and maintain a plane. Before he could solo, his instructor left town for another job. In order to earn some money, Lindbergh joined a pilot named H. J. Lynch for a season of barnstorming. Lindbergh walked the wings as they flew over a new town to advertise their act. He also made trick parachute jumps, but never flew the plane.

Finally he bought a Curtiss Jenny of his own and soloed. Then he began barnstorming again. He liked the life, sleeping under the upper wing in a hammock, traveling light with nothing more than a razor and a toothbrush, and taking people up in his plane for their first ride. Lindbergh quit barnstorming in 1924 because there had been too many accidents and joined the U. S. Air Service, flying mail around the country. In the years to come, Lindbergh would become one of the most influential and celebrated pilots in the history of aviation.

In the meantime, barnstormers continued to be hurt and killed, and newspapers across the nation increased their opposition to the reckless activity. Commercially employed pilots and aircraft builders began to listen and react. They wanted to showcase aviation as a reliable and useful method of transportation. By contrast, the

Charles Lindbergh (in goggles), as an airmail pilot in 1926, loads a sack of mail into his plane.

barnstormers were emphasizing its risks and limitations.

By the mid-twenties, the first barnstormers had either gone on to safer jobs in the industry or been killed. New, younger pilots replacing them found it increasingly difficult to find audiences or passengers. Barnstorming by individual pilots dramatically declined after the U.S. Congress passed the Air Commerce Act of 1926. The act specified that it would license all pilots and mechanics, register and certify aircraft, and regulate air traffic. The government, however, still couldn't restrict the numbers of daredevils who wanted to fly. So the era of the flying circus was born.

This stunt pilot had to adjust for the weight of the stuntman hanging beneath the tail of the plane.

The Flying Circus

Flying circuses were made up of groups of barnstormers who more or less complied with the Air Commerce Act. One of the original groups, the Gates Flying Circus, employed eleven young pilots specializing in aerial antics such as flying upside down. This stunt was especially tricky because the Jenny's engine depended on gravity for the flow of fuel to the engine. It barely idled when inverted. Another popular flying maneuver required pilots to loop around each other in tight formation.

The circuses also had specialists in *dead stick landings,* changing planes in midair, and wing-walking. Like solo barnstormers, the flying circuses attracted attention by buzzing rooftops along the main streets of small towns across the nation and persuading an audience to follow them to a nearby field. It was difficult, however, to get

A stuntman dives from a Jenny into water below.

Gladys Engle, a famous female aerialist of her day, prepares to climb from the wing of one Jenny to another in mid-flight.

the entire audience to pay admission when they could stand across the street and see the show free of charge.

As flying circuses increased in number, they challenged one another to perform the most unusual or scariest stunts to attract larger audiences. Roy Ahearn of the Tidewater Air Circus bought an old Jenny, tied sacks of gunpowder to it, poured oil and gasoline on its wings, and set it aflame in the night sky. He escaped by parachute. Eddie Angel performed an act called "the dive of death," in which he jumped out of a plane after dark. With a flashlight in each hand, he opened his parachute only after he could see the ground. Walter Hunter hung by his knees underneath a plane, and then dropped into a haystack without any parachute at all.

Mabel Cody, niece of Buffalo Bill Cody, was one of the first women to enter this dangerous occupation. She organized her own flying circus and surrounded herself with such stunt people as Bonnie Rowe, who made a plane change with one hand tied behind him. Mabel specialized in delayed parachute jumps, danced on the wings, and moved from speedboat to aircraft with ease.

Doug Davis, another circus owner, often vied with Mabel for the same audiences at the same time. Their rivalry became so intense that one day they settled it in

Mabel Cody jumps from a speedboat to a ladder attached to a Jenny above.

the sky. For ten minutes they put on the wildest performance ever seen—looping, flipping, and snap-rolling through the air as Doug tried to shake Mabel off his tail. Finally he thought he'd figured out one place where she wouldn't go and landed his plane on an empty flatcar of a moving train. Mabel landed on a freight car just behind him, proving she could do anything he could do. Soon they merged their circuses under one banner and became the most famous barnstorming troupe of their day.

Even with the Department of Commerce regulating the rules it had established, there were still too many accidents and deaths, so additional restrictions were placed on the aerial daredevils. Pilots were forbidden to carry explosives or fireworks, fly within 300 feet (91 m) of each other, or operate without lights from unlighted fields. Airplanes would be grounded if they did not meet the new standards. "We're going to make it safe for everyone to fly," one inspector said.

New aerial circuses entered the scene by 1929. They were different from the pioneer performers as they bought new, more dependable aircraft and maintained strict control over their upkeep. The 13 Black Cats adhered to restrictions, even regulating their prices for certain acts. They charged $450 to perform a loop with a man standing on each wing. A fight on the upper wing cost $225 dollars, and a head-on collision with automobiles cost a little more at $250. Even the owner's dog,

Chandelle, logged a thousand hours of flight time in her own act.

Not to be outdone, the Flying Aces starred stray cats in their show. Launching them from planes by miniature parachute, the cats were quickly adopted by members of the audience as a kind of bonus prize for attendance.

Inspectors and regulators continued to haunt the air circuses, restricting activities until many were forced to close down. Years later, a former air circus owner stated, "What they [the government] did not realize was that there would not have been any airlines if there had not been people like us. We kept aviation before the eyes of the public and showed airplanes and flying to people all over the country who otherwise might not have even been aware that airplanes existed."

Members of the 13 Black Cats, a flying circus of the 1920s, perform on the wing of a Jenny.

3
SKY SCIENCE

Not every aviator who came home from the battle-fields of World War I wanted to be a barnstormer, daring fate and his fragile aircraft to keep him in the air. World War I had provided the push needed for the engineering and development of airplanes, but pilot safety had taken a back seat. Back home, the returning pilots hoped to change that. They wanted their aircraft to travel faster, but they also preferred to get where they were going in one piece. They started small companies to push aviation ahead in those areas.

The public provided another impetus. Any new advance, any new adventure was applauded by the fascinated public. World War I had given the public its share of wartime heroes. Now peacetime heroes were needed, fast. New records needed to be broken, new first flights made, races won. So the air shows revved up once again and became extremely popular. Heroes of sky science were quickly born. The potential of aviation was about to be expanded from one horizon to the other.

Before World War I, international air racing had been conducted as a kind of gentlemanly sport. After the war, things changed dramatically. Governments around the world competed for peacetime supremacy of the sky, and the United States still lagged behind the nations of Europe. It needed to catch up quickly.

Power came first. Most of the planes prior to the war had been powered by engines similar in size to automobile engines. As the shape of the plane changed, becoming more streamlined, the engine changed too, becoming more complex and powerful.

The Need for Speed

An American engineer named Charles Nutt designed the CD-12 engine (CD for Curtiss Direct Drive), which he installed in two Navy pursuit planes. They would be flown by military test pilots in the new Pulitzer Trophy air race sponsored by the newspaper publishing Pulitzer brothers.

The public was ready. More than 40,000 spectators had gathered at Mitchell Field in Garden City, Long Island, 24 hours before the start of the first Pulitzer race on Thanksgiving Day, November 20, 1920. Although the Navy's planes did not compete well, the race was con-

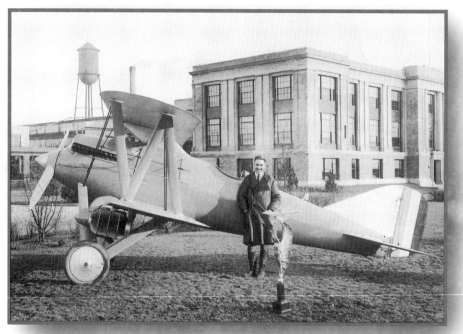

Bert Acosta poses in front of the airplane in which he won the 1921 Pulitzer Trophy race. The Pulitzer Trophy stands in the foreground.

sidered a success. Glenn Curtiss said after it was over, "The public, at last, is interested in airplanes." The government, too, was now interested. In order to exert a tighter control over this new national craze, the government established the National Aeronautical Association.

American engineers and designers went to work immediately to build a better, faster plane for the next race. The result was a sleek little biplane built by Glenn

Curtiss's company in just two months. With it, Bert Acosta of the Navy established a new world record for closed-circuit racing at 176.7 miles (284.3 km) per hour.

New design ideas were submitted to the Navy but, surprisingly, they were turned down. Within a few months, however, the Army agreed to sponsor the new designs. More complex than any shown before, these Curtiss racers also turned out to be the fastest yet built, clocking in at 200 (322 km) miles per hour.

The international racing world grew curious about these radical new designs and bought several of them to see how they worked. Over the next several years, Curtiss racers continued to break speed records everywhere. It soon became obvious to those in aviation that the more money spent in development and research, the better the airplane.

In 1925, a new name began to win recognition by the public. James Doolittle had earned one of the first doctorates in aeronautics, but his piloting feats quickly overshadowed his academic accomplishments. He won races, set records, and later, during World War II, he would lead an air raid against Tokyo, Japan, and become one of the war's most decorated heroes. In the twenties, however, Doolittle and other pilots were doing what they could to keep the nation's attention on safe flying.

Charles Lindbergh (second from right of banner) poses in front of his plane, the *Spirit of St. Louis,* before embarking on his record-setting solo flight from New York to Paris.

Then, on May 20, 1927, Charles Lindbergh made a record-setting solo flight across the Atlantic Ocean to Paris, France. His flight was celebrated throughout the United States and Europe, and he became one of the world's biggest celebrities. With this single flight, Lindbergh refocused public enthusiasm on aviation. Suddenly, the world seemed smaller as people realized that traveling across oceans by air was a real possibility. Lindbergh said that his flight wasn't about money but "to advance the cause of aviation." And he did just that.

The Cleveland National Air Races

The mood was right, and the stage was set for a group of promoters to sponsor a national air race and aeronautical exposition in Cleveland, Ohio. On August 27, 1929, 80,000 spectators jammed the city to see the exhibits and air show.

An official program from the 1929 National Air Races in Cleveland

Activity centered at the newly remodeled Cleveland airport. Innovative competitions dominated the event, such as a women's air race between Santa Monica, California, and Cleveland. Prominent pilots, including Charles Lindbergh in a Navy plane, demonstrated tactical maneuvers and *aerobatics*. There were glider races, blimp races, and even pigeon races. Other events included parachute jumping and balloon bursting. Each evening, fireworks displays, night-flying demonstrations, and musical extravaganzas entertained the record-breaking audiences.

The promoters saved the best for last. The final race, on a 50-mile (80.5-km) closed course, pitted civilian planes against the best that the armed forces could put in the air. Everyone assumed the military planes would win. The Army and Navy planes were Curtiss Hawks—a new plane from Glenn Curtiss—modified especially for this race.

One of the civilian planes, the Vega, had been designed by a self-educated engineer named John K. Northrop. The other civilian plane, the Mystery, had been designed by two engineers in Walter Beech's Travel Air Company. It was called the Mystery because the designers kept the plane hidden in a hangar and wrapped in tarpaulins before the event began.

It was no contest. In a field of eleven entries, the *Mystery*, piloted by Doug Davis of flying circus fame,

Doug Davies taxies in his plane, the *Mystery*, after his upset win of the final race at the 1929 National Air Races.

came in first, the Vega third, upsetting what was expected to be a contest between military planes.

Culminating seven days of innovative flying, this one race ushered in a new era in which the "shade-tree" mechanic—the designer-aviator who worked in his backyard or small shop—became one of the most important contributors to aeronautics.

4
SPEED
KINGS GO
TO WAR

I n 1911, a pilot named Calbraith P. Rodgers became the first person to fly across the United States. On the way west, he ran into trees and fences, thunderstorms and chicken coops, and put up with exploding engines. Nearly every original part of his airplane had been replaced by the time he landed. Rodgers took forty-nine days to fly from Sheepshead Bay, Long Island, to Pasadena, California, and even longer to reach his own goal at the ocean's edge. Over the years that followed, other pilots crossed the United States in less time as cows, chickens, and a few interested fans of aviation looked on.

In 1931, Vincent Bendix, president of the Bendix Aviation Corporation, established the first organized transcontinental race. He offered a trophy and cash as a reward to the pilot who crossed the United States in

Calbraith P. Rogers flies low over a field during his 1911 flight across the United States.

the fastest time, and the race was on. James Doolittle won the first Bendix Trophy with a time of a little more than eleven hours.

The Bendix Trophy race became one of the most popular air races of the 1930s. Safety and design continued to be foremost in the minds of all participants. By 1938, the carefree days of barnstorming were rapidly drawing to a close as the new Civil Aeronautics Act regulated flying so closely that it grounded the daredevils of the past.

James Doolitle sits in the cockpit of his airplane after winning the Bendix Trophy in 1931.

Another World War

The world of aviation changed even more the following year. In the summer of 1939, final preparations were underway for another National Air Race in Cleveland to be held during the end of August and beginning of September. Participants were preoccupied; in fact, the mood of the entire nation was somber and watchful as the clouds of war gathered in Europe. In the qualifying trials for one race, conducted several days before the official opening, a pilot was killed. At that moment, the fun all but disappeared from the gathering.

And then it happened. On September 1, word was received that Germany had invaded Poland and World War II had begun. The pilots, designers, and airplane manufacturers gathered in Cleveland knew their lives were about to change. Trophies were won, records broken, and new heroes made in this National Air Race, but the participants suddenly had more serious things to think about.

During World War II, the United States produced more than 300,000 airplanes. Pictured here, women workers polish the nose cones of airplanes on an assembly line. The shiny nose cones reflect the factory lights above.

Although the United States didn't enter the war until December 8, 1941, the country's leaders already realized that airpower had suddenly become all-important to national security. As the United States prepared for eventual war, former stunt pilots and speed kings of the American skies enlisted in the military, ready to train recruits, fly, or even build planes.

By early 1942, the United States and its allies were planning an air offensive over Europe. Personnel, supplies, and planes were ferried across the Atlantic Ocean. Meanwhile, the United States manufactured airplanes. By the end of the war, American technology had built more than 300,000 of them.

Slowly, the *Allies* gained control of the skies over Europe. Small fighter planes looped and rolled through the sky while protecting the heavier bombers on deadly raids over Germany. In the Allied invasion of Europe on June 6, 1944, more than eleven thousand aircraft of every kind took part in the massive assault. The war ended in Europe in May 1945, and in the Pacific against Japan in August of the same year.

Aeronautical technology progressed significantly during World War II. Nevertheless, the war was fought and won primarily with technology developed before 1939. Technologies such as piston engines, turbochargers, and pressurization were largely developed by the shade-tree mechanics and manufacturers of old. Even radar was utilized before the war. Although jet engines and computer gunsights were introduced during the war, complete development of these technologies waited until war's end.

After the War

National air races and private air shows returned very slowly after the war. Cleveland held the first postwar races in the United States in 1946. Planes broke records

After World War II, the National Air Races resumed in Cleveland. Pictured here, a large crowd watches an airplane race in 1949.

Two stunt pilots practice for the Miami Air Maneuvers in 1939. This air show was unable to be revived after World War II.

in each event because they were much more powerful than the custom-built racers of pre-war days. Fighters such as P-51s, Mustangs, and Corsairs could be purchased for as little as one thousand dollars, then modified to race in air shows.

The Miami All-American Air Maneuvers was organized in 1929. After World War II ended, organizers tried to hold the Maneuvers again, but the skies over Miami became so congested that the show was canceled for good. General Claire Chennault, who had gained fame locally in the early shows, grew into national prominence during World War II when he organized a group called the Flying Tigers.

The Cole Brothers Air Show had been one of the earlier flying circuses. Now the Coles re-entered the air show scene after the war, performing comedy acts and flying vintage planes from the twenties and thirties. Most of the other shows were military-dominated.

In 1952, a pilot coming to a show in Flager, Colorado (as a spectator, not a participant), performed a roll as he flew over the field. Suddenly his plane flew out of control and crashed into the crowd, injuring many and killing a number of spectators. The Civil Aeronautics Association immediately stopped all air shows until an investigation was conducted and new rules established.

When the International Council of Air Shows was established in 1968, it provided a means for sponsors and participants to get together and organize public events. The air-show entertainment industry began to grow rapidly. Air shows had come of age, again!

5
FESTIVALS IN THE SKY

Today's performers carry on the tradition of the barnstormers, but with a difference. Once the International Council of Air Shows (ICAS) was organized in 1968, these events evolved into a showcase of modern aviation and highly skilled pilots. Both individuals and the industry were now bound by a code of ethics as well as federal rules and regulations structured to safeguard both participants and fans.

On most weekends from April through September, an air show is going on at a nearby airport. It may be as small as a group of pilots gathered in a hangar, entertaining themselves and a small crowd by swapping stories as they fly with their hands. Or it may be a three-day, five-star benefit using the most modern technology. For the average price of a movie and a bag of popcorn, the spectator can count on a full day of excitement and education as the nation's top pilots loop and spin against the backdrop of a lazy summer sky.

People of all ages attend an air show in Lakeland, Florida.

No one knows exactly how many air shows take place throughout the nation during any given year. Officials of the ICAS state that the number of air shows each year is approximately 450. Paid-attendance figures indicate that air shows are second in popularity only to major-league baseball games.

This popularity has not been lost on corporations who want to sell their products, nor on charity organizations who need to raise money for worthwhile causes. Each year more businesses become involved through sponsorship of individual performers or acrobatic teams whose

An air show reproduction of a German World War I fighter plane.

airplanes whiz by as flying billboards. Corporate sponsorship dates back at least to Calbraith Rodgers's 1911 flight across the United States. He was sponsored by Vin Fiz, a popular grape drink that cost five cents a bottle.

Most air shows donate some of their revenues to charitable organizations. The Salinas, California, air show pioneered the concept of finding sponsors among local businesses to underwrite the cost of the show. Excess funds from ticket sales then became available to donate to charitable organizations. Other air shows, such as the one held in Yakima, Washington, pledge scholarship money to aid deserving students. The ICAS estimates

The Red Arrows, the precision flying group of the Britain's Royal Air Force

that, in one year alone, more than $16 million was donated to charities nationwide.

Entire communities benefit from air shows, too. Abbotsford, British Columbia, is a little-known, small town east of Vancouver that holds one of the largest air events in Canada. For three days each year, it attracts tens of thousands of visitors to the area from all over the world to feast their eyes on events in the sky and exhibits on the ground. A

Biplanes performing stunts at the Abbotsford, British Columbia, air show

trade show and aerospace conference is part of the package, showcasing every high-tech, state-of-the-art gadget known to the flying world.

Oshkosh, Wisconsin, used to be known strictly for its overalls. Now, it attracts aviation fans from across the globe. Each year the Experimental Aircraft Association holds the largest convention and air show of its kind here in this typical midwestern town. During an average event, which lasts for one week, as many as 800,000 people from around the world gather to see what's new as well as greet old friends and make new ones. Approximately

This annual air show in Oshkosh, Wisconsin, is one of the largest of its kind.

15,000 airplanes will fly in and out of the Oshkosh airport before the air show is finished.

Aerobatics

As air shows have grown and matured, piloting skills have become more precise and exact. Advances in technology have resulted in stronger, lighter planes that allow pilots to perform well-executed maneuvers. Many highly skilled pilots have been trained in the sport of acrobatic competition.

If a pilot wants to compete in aerobatics, he or she will first have to learn technique from a qualified teacher. The first thing to be learned is precise control of the aircraft. That's what everyone, from acrobatic champions to air-show heroes, looks for in newcomers as well as in their own performances.

All air show performers look for perfection. This attitude separates reckless daredevils from air-show artists. The responsible pilot soon knows the limitations

Stunt pilots fly special planes designed to withstand the strong forces put on a plane by aerobatic flying.

of his own skill as well as that of his aircraft. When a pilot can put together a spin-loop-roll sequence with reasonable control, he is eligible for the first of ten achievement awards given by the International Aerobatic Club (IAC). A spin, a loop, and a roll are three basic aerobatic figures, or maneuvers. A spin-loop-roll sequence means these figures are performed one after the other, as a unit. Usually this spin-loop-roll maneuver can be achieved after a couple of weekends of practice.

Stunt pilots are pushed and pulled in many directions as they loop through the air. Many beginning pilots experience motion sickness as they adjust to the new sensations.

If the pilot wants to measure his skill against others, he can then enter one of approximately forty-five sanctioned IAC events held throughout the year. There are five levels of competition. All levels demand precise speed, timing, and altitude control, as well as calculations for wind and temperature. All maneuvers must be performed in an acrobatic zone over the airport called a box. This is a block of air space 3,300 feet (1,000 m) long, 3,300 feet (1,000 m) wide, with a top altitude of 3,500 feet (1,067 m) for most pilots and a top altitude of 3,280 feet

(995 m) for the most advanced pilots. The bottom altitude is set at 1,500 feet (457 m) above the ground for less skilled pilots and 328 feet (100 m) for the most skilled.

Competition flights are graded by a team of five judges. They grade on such factors as precision of line and angle, symmetry of figures, and how well the sequence is positioned in the box. Other factors are contained in the official contest rules. Each judge has a copy of the figures the pilot will fly.

The competition categories are: basic and sportsman, intermediate, advanced, and unlimited. In the basic category, every pilot flies the same set of figures, called known figures. These are published by the International Aerobatic Club before the contest season begins, hence the name. All entrants in categories higher than sportsman fly known figures as well as unknown figures. Participants do not know what the unknown figures will be until the competition begins and do not have an opportunity to practice them.

In the unlimited category of competition, the pilot has reached the ultimate, most difficult category. By this time pilots have polished their skills and compete with the most experienced competitors. The pilot must fly an extremely high-performance aircraft capable of flying the demanding figures required. In addition to the known and unknown figures, pilots in the unlimited category also fly a four-minute free program. During the four-minute free competition, pilots fly figures of their own choosing. This part of the contest is especially exciting and entertaining.

Organized in 1953, the sport of aerobatics is relatively new to flying and didn't get off the ground right away. Yet, the interest and excitement it has generated since the seventies indicates it will continue to grow in popularity both as a spectator and participant sport.

Precision Flying Groups

There are many performers in this sport, both individuals and groups, who are popular throughout the United States, Canada, and the world. One of the most famous

The Canadian Snowbirds approach in tight formation.

The undersides of the Thunderbirds are painted to give the impression of wings.

groups, the Canadian Snowbirds, recently celebrated 25 years of performing and are as popular today as they were when they began. Chosen for their excellence and reliability, members of the group are drawn from the Royal Canadian Air Force.

Twinkling lights on their nine airplanes appear in the distance as their performance begins. While they perform their intricate opening maneuvers, a microphone in the cockpit allows the audience to hear the team leader call commands for the maneuvers as they occur.

The team then proceeds through graceful demonstrations featuring all nine aircraft. Then, one or two solo pilots perform fast-paced, exciting maneuvers. After the solos, formations of five and seven planes perform aerial ballets to music accompaniment. Some of the maneuvers have become classics, such as the "Big Diamond Roll," the "Inverted Wedge Turnaround," and "Maple Leaf Split." All sequences are designed to keep the entire display in full view of the audience at all time.

The Thunderbirds, a U.S. Air Force team, is similar to the Snowbirds. Organized in 1953, the team has performed all over the world, and continues to thrill and amaze spectators with its precision flying. Beginning in March, the six-pilot team tours the United States, and often the world as well, flying at least 60 shows in F-16S fighter planes. Their tour ends in November when they return to their home base at Nellis Air Force base in Nevada. Of the six pilots, two fly as soloists during their show. All perform such figures as crossovers, line abreast loops, and five-card loops.

The Blue Angels, the U. S. Navy and Marine Corps precision flying group, was founded in 1946 by Admiral Chester Nimitz to promote continued interest in this kind of flying. Lt. Butch Voris was the first lead pilot. Today the configuration in the air is similar to the Thunderbirds, with six pilots in the air, two of whom fly as soloists

Pilots in the Blue Angels undergo extensive training before they are safely able to fly so close together.

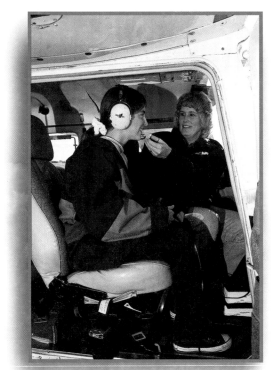

At air shows, spectators are allowed inside many of the planes. For some young people, this is where dreams of becoming a pilot begin.

during the show. In 1991, the Blue Angels became the first precision group to fly in Russia.

When not performing, the Thunderbirds and the Blue Angels visit hospitals and schools to talk about their adventures in the air. Every Tuesday morning from April to November, the public is invited to attend over-the-field practice sessions by the Blue Angels at their home base—Sherman Field in Pensacola, Florida.

Through the years, air shows and aerobatics have continued to provide a source of inspiration for the public who come out to see the exciting festivals of the sky. Young people find the shows particularly impressive. They not only watch but are allowed to touch the planes, talk to the pilots, and even sit in, climb on, and walk through the aircraft on display. In those moments, dreams of flying airplanes begin. For some, the dreams will one day become a reality.

Glossary

aerobatics—performing loops, spins, rolls, and other acrobatic maneuvers in an airplane

aeronautics—the science of flight

Allies—the countries that opposed Germany, Japan, and Italy during World War II. The major Allied powers were the United States, Britain, and the Soviet Union.

buzzing—flying an airplane very low over the ground

dead stick landing—landing without power when the engine is turned off. The plane effectively becomes a glider.

piston engine—engine driven by pistons, which are disks or cylinders that move within a tube and exert pressure on fluid inside the tube.

pressurization—maintaining normal air pressure inside an airplane while flying at high altitudes

radar—device that uses radio waves to locate an object

turbocharger—a device that compresses the intake air to get more horsepower from an engine

For More Information

Books

Crisfield, Deborah. *Air Show Adventure*. Mahwah, NJ: Troll Communications, 1990.

Hart, Philip S. *Flying Free: America's First Black Aviators*. Minneapolis: Lerner Publications, Co., 1996.

Jefferis, David. *Flight: Flyers and Flying Machines*. New York: Franklin Watts, 1991.

Stein, R. Conrad. *The Spirit of St. Louis*. Chicago: Children's Press, 1994.

Taylor, Richard L. *The First Flight: The Story of the Wright Brothers*. New York: Franklin Watts, 1990.

Tessendorf, K. C. *Barnstormers and Daredevils*. New York: Simon & Schuster, 1988.

Internet Resources

Enduring Heritage
http://www.thehistorynet.com/AviationHistory/articles/05962_text.htm
This page describes the accomplishments of aviation pioneer Glenn Curtiss.

Experimental Aircraft Association (EAA)
http://www.eaa.org/
This is the home of the organization that sponsors the annual air show in Oshkosh, Wisconsin. EAA is dedicated to promoting the interests of individuals in the world of flight. Check out the Young Eagles link to find out about their program for giving free flights to young people.

First Flight Shrine
http://www.firstflight.org/shrine/
This site contains a series of short biographies of the most important figures in the history of aviation.

International Aerobatic Club (IAC)
http://acro.harvard.edu/IAC/
This site offers images and other information on aerobatic flying. This is a great place to learn more about becoming an aerobatic pilot. International Council of Air Shows (ICAS)

The World Federation of Air Show Congress
http://members.aol.com/KCAIRSHOW/page2.html
This site offers lots of information on air shows including specific pages on the Blue Angels and Thunderbirds.

Index

Page numbers in italics indicate photographs.

About the Author

Elizabeth Van Steenwyk has written more than fifty books for young people, including the Franklin Watts First Books *The California Missions, Frederic Remington, The California Gold Rush: West with the Forty-Niners,* and *Saddlebag Salesmen*. She also wrote *Ida B. Wells-Barnett: Woman of Courage,* which was a NCSS/CBC Notable Children's Trade Book in the Field of Social Studies for 1992. Ms. Van Steenwyk lives with her husband in San Marino, California.